SUPER EAGLE

A FIERY BEGINNING

Joe Lyon

Illustrated by Stephen Adams

authorHOUSE®

AuthorHouse™
1663 Liberty Drive
Bloomington, IN 47403
www.authorhouse.com
Phone: 1-800-839-8640

First published by AuthorHouse 4/17/2009

ISBN: 978-1-4389-7497-2 (sc)

Printed in the United States of America
Bloomington, Indiana

This book is printed on acid-free paper.

CONTENTS

CHAPTER 1
STOPPING AN ASSASSIN,
STARTING AN ADVENTURE

Neuva Libre City, a sprawling metropolis, and the capitol of the Central American nation of Neuva Libre. Many high-rise skyscrapers dot the center of town and the network of roads bustles with traffic. Sitting at the center of this bustling, modern metropolitan area is the Ministry of Commerce Building.

Sitting atop the peak of the building, a small cluster of offices, surrounded by a beautiful patio area that is set up for a brunch. It's there that Alexa Mayhew, a tall lanky young lady stands at the railing. She seems unusually thin, yet very muscular. Arthur Mayhew, tall, prematurely gray and a bit heavier than he should be, stand with her.

Out on the patio steps the Minister of Commerce short yet distinguished man. He smiles and moves toward Alexa and Arthur.

"Senor Mayhew, come, you and your daughter are to be my honored guests today."

Arthur gives him a small nod. "Thank you, sir. You honor us."

"It is the least we can do. Your new factory means many jobs for our people."

"All due to my Alexa; she picked out the site."

Alexa turns to the Minister, a smile on hers face. A flash of light appears off in the distance, over the Minister's shoulder. Alexa focuses on the spot, her eye acts like a zoom lens and she studies a distant building. There, off in an open window of the building, she sees a high-powered rifle with a sniper's scope pointing toward them.

"Oh... it was... nothing. Such a beautiful place... deserves help," she says, even as she reaches into her coat pocket. Her cellphone rings. "Oh, my phone. Would you excuse me a moment?"

The Minister nods. "Of course. Senor Mayhew, shall we be seated?"

"Yes," Arthur replied. "Alexa, don't be long."

"Be back before you know it!" she says.

Arthur and the Minister move to the table and sit. The waiters move in to fill their glasses. Alexa dashes inside, and then comes out on the other side of the patio a moment later. She moves to the railing, looks around to be sure no one is watching, and jumps. She casts off her suit jacket and shirt, and transforms into Super Eagle! Spreading her wings, she flies off.

Nearby, a small sparsely furnished room, bed, dresser, table and chair. A corner apartment, it has windows in the two outer walls. A young man, short and stocky sits in the chair by the window and holds a rifle.

From his clothes and appearance, he looks like a stereotype South American rebel. He sights through the scope and prepares to fire. Alexa, dressed as Super Eagle, swoops in the other window and lands next to the bed.

The assassin, startled, turns to face her. "Sacre blu! Who, what are you?" he says, in a thick French accent.

"Super Eagle, Defender of Justice! Cease your act of violence."

"I think not, you-you... overstuffed pigeon!"

He swings the rifle around and goes to point it at Alexa. She hurls a feature-shaped dart at him. It strikes him in the chest; he staggers, stumbles and drops the rifle. He pulls out the dart, looks at Alexa, and passes out. Alexa moves forward, ties the assassin up, and searches the room. She finds a picture of the minister and some cigarettes, but nothing else.

Moving to the window, she prepares to fly off, then notices a car parked in the street below with its engine running. Alexa focuses on the car. She sees a Land Rover parked on a narrow road. Two airplane tickets can be seen through the windshield, and Greg Grimm, a big hulking thug of a man sits behind the wheel. He leans out the window and looks up. He sees Alexa, pulls his head back in and races off.

Alexa, unsure of what this all means, flies off back toward the ministry building.

Later, in the Mayhew's private sleek, modern high-tech jet, Arthur and Alexa sit facing each other over a small table. Arthur types on a laptop while Alexa draws on a note pad.

"You sure the tickets were for today on Trans-Global Airlines?" Arthur says.

"Yeah, Pop, I'm positive. What, you having trouble hacking into their system?"

Arthur snorts. "I'm going to try and forget you said that. Ah, here we are! Oh, we got some comedians at work here."

"Why do you say that?"

"A Mr. Tom Collins and a Mr. Harvey Wallbanger have tickets to New York today. And... ah, their tickets were bought by Globe-Corp."

Alexa chews her lip. "Hmmm... what is going on? Someone went to a lot of trouble to make it look like the rebels were out to kill the Minister."

"What makes you think he wasn't a rebel assassin?"

"Well, he was smoking Turkish cigarettes, he spoke French, and he was using a rifle that cost more than the rebels spent on their whole army!"

Arthur's brow wrinkles. "You sure?"

Alexa nods. "Yeah, I saw the same gun on the Discovery Channel. They had a program about military sniper assassins."

"Ah, I see. What you got there?" he asks, indicating the pad.

Alexa holds up the picture he's drawn of the car driver. "It's the man from the car. Right now, he's our chief lead."

"Ah, you have your mother's hands."

"That's fine, just so long as I don't end up with her figure!"

Hours later, the plane flies over Eagle Island; a small, lush green island with rolling hills. A quaint village sits nestled around a little harbor. A lighthouse stands at the tip of a stone jetty; it and its mate mark the entrance to the harbor.

Once they land at the small airport, it's a short drive home. Inside, the living room is a dazzling, ultra-modern split level room. Beautiful oil paintings line the wall. Over the huge stone fireplace is a family portrait: Arthur, Alexa, Silvana and Alexa's younger sister, Katrina.

Near the window is an artist's easel. Silvana Mayhew, a tall, willowy Italian beauty with long blond hair and green eyes stands at the easel and paints. Alexa enters, crosses to Silvana, and gives her a quick peck on the cheek.

"Hey, Mom, how's it going? That what you're going to enter in the art festival?"

Silvana nods. "Yes, along with a couple others. What do you think?"

"You look great, but Bratina's eyes should be redder."

"Alexa, stop calling your sister that! You know it upsets her."

"Yeah, you're right. Why waste a perfectly good insult when she's not here to hear it?"

Silvana smacks her in the back of the head. "Alexa!"

"Okay-okay. I'm going to... unpack, it was a long trip."

"Good idea. Where's your father?"

"Where else? His lab."

Silvana sighs. "Oh, why can't that man ever learn to relax? Did you eat enough on your trip? You look thin."

"Yeah, I gnawed on a dry peanut on the flight back."

"Alexa! Why not eat something now? I just baked from fresh banana bread."

"Ohhh, my favorite. But, we're going to have dinner in an hour."

"Yes, but you should still eat something."

Alexa rolls his eyes. "What - ever."

Alexa heads out of the room, and down the wide hallway. At the far end of the spacious house is her equally spacious bedroom; decked out with family photos, science contest awards (all first place) and lots of eagle memorabilia: posters, pictures, statues etc. Sliding glass doors give access to a deck area. She tosses hers jacket and suitcase onto the bed.

She pats an eagle statue, steps over to the far wall and turns the head of another eagle statue. The wall opens, revealing a secret room, and she goes in. in side is the ultimate in high-tech science. Computers, lab equipment, books and all of Alexa's Super Eagle gear are carefully arranged throughout the room. A huge electronic eye hangs from the center of the room. It is the visual center of the lab's super computer: HEuristic Intelligent Data Integrator

"Hello, Alexa, I am pleased to see you safely home," says a voice.

"Hello, HEIDI, good to see you too," she says, waving at the electronic eye.

"You look thin. Did you eat enough on your trip?"

Alexa rolls her eyes. "HEIDI, give it a rest, huh? I get enough of that from Mom. Now, I've got a job for you."

She pulls out the picture she drew on the plane and places it in a scanner.

"Hmmm, quite the dashing fellow, but, he has mean eyes. You want an ident on him?"

"You got it. See if you can hack into the personnel files at Globe-Corp. Think you handle that?"

"Humph! I am going to try and delete that comment from my memory files."

Alexa laughs. "Sorry, HEIDI. You find anything, buzz me. Dad and I are jetting out to New York tomorrow."

"So soon? You have only just returned. There is the matter of the art festival. You had intended-"

"Yes, I know, I was going to enter my drawings! Well... something's come up. I got a feeling there's a problem with the new factory. Also, find out all you can about the rebels in Neuva Libre. I want to know if Globe-Corp is connected to them in any way!"

5

"As you wish, Alexa. I will devote all my runtime to the assignments."

The next day, Alexa and Arthur jet down to New York City; the Big Apple. Cloud-piercing skyscrapers dot the Island of Manhattan. Their jet swoops low in the sky as it angles to land at JFK International Airport.

Later, outside the office building of Globe-Corp, an ultra-modern building of glass and steel that dwarfs all of the surrounding buildings,

Alexa and Arthur, dressed in their best business suits and carrying briefcases, enter.

From the lobby, they enter the elevator. Alexa watches the different numbers of the floors light up. The number "13" is missing from the list.

The elevator stops, and the doors open at the twelfth floor. After they check in with the receptionist, they move into the conference room; a large round room, one wall of it is glass and looks out over the city. A huge oval mahogany table dominates the center of the room.

Alexa stands by the window and carefully studies the room. Arthur sits at the table and lays out papers from his briefcase. Alexa suddenly stiffens and turns his ear toward the door.

"Someone's coming down a flight of stairs behind that wall."

"Maybe it's our host. Remember, we're here to discuss business! So, let's play it cool."

"Pop, if I can jump off a building, I can play it cool."

"Oh, yeah, right."

The door opens, and Kelly Delaney, tall, attractive and dressed for business enters. She shakes each of their hands.

"Mister Mayhew, it's a pleasure to meet you and Alexa; I've heard so much about you."

Arthur smiles. "Thank you, Miss Delaney. When we spoke on the phone yesterday, I had no idea you were so attractive."

"Dad!"

Kelly laughs. "It's quite all right, Alexa. Your father is just using one of the oldest negotiating techniques there is: flattery. So, you're looking to expand your South American operation and need financing. What, you 'bite off more than you can chew', is that it?"

Arthur smiles and gestures toward the papers. "Not at all. If you'll just take a look at these records, you'll see how profitable investing in Neuva Libre can be. Plus, there's-"

"No, I don't think so! GC has no interest in that country."

Alexa's brow wrinkles. "Really? So, you have no... personnel down there?"

"Of course not! Is that the only project you're looking for investment in?"

Arthur shakes his head. "Of course not. Sit, please, we'll show you are full portfolio."

Some times later, back outside the building, Arthur sits on a bench and shuffles papers in his briefcase. Alexa stands and looks up at the building. The sun hangs low in the sky; night is little more than an hour away.

"Well, that was a waste of an afternoon," Arthur grumbles.

"I don't think so. You remember, she came down a flight of stairs to meet with us?"

"Yeah. So? Maybe she doesn't like elevators."

"We met on the twelfth floor, and the elevator didn't list a thirteenth. So, she came from that floor."

"That's normal; a lot of people are afraid of the number thirteen. Interesting story behind the origins of that. It all goes back to-"

"Pop, focus! The elevator showed thirty floors, skipping thirteen. That means the building should be twenty-nine stories high. I just counted. It's thirty stories."

"Ah! Which means, they've got a thirteenth floor, it's just hidden. Hmmm... I'm willing to bet the elevator doesn't even stop there, and it's probably bristling with security."

Alexa grins. "Right. So, tonight, I'll pay them a little visit."

"Alexa, you think you should? I mean, getting into a high security place that like could be tough."

She laughs. "You call it tough, I call it fun!"

Later that night, the full moon dominates the star-filled sky. Alexa, dressed as Super Eagle, is seen in silhouette as she flutters across the sky and closes in on the building. A line shoots out from her belt and attaches to a window of the thirteenth floor. She hovers near the building. The line shimmers and vibrates. The window rattles, and then shatters.

Alexa flies in through the opening and lands in a store room; reams of paper stacks on wire racks, toner cartridges, boxes of pens etc. She moves to the door and opens it. The hall is dimly lit, and a security camera swings back and forth, scanning the area. Alexa sticks her head out into the hall and looks about.

Alexa focuses her eagle-like vision on the floor and sees lingering thermal footprints on the carpet. The brightest ones, left by a woman's shoes, leave a path to an office at the far end of the hall. Seeing the camera, she whips out a small device from her belt and aims it at the camera.

BUZZ. The camera stops moving. Alexa darts out the door, down the hall and into the office at the far end. A moment later, the camera starts to work again.

Alexa finds herself in Kelly's office; a large, spacious office dominated by a massive desk. Locked file cabinets are against the wall opposite the floor to ceiling window, and pictures of Kelly dot the room.

Alexa stands at the door and scans the room. She moves to the file cabinets and sees one labeled: "Central American Operation." Using a small device, she picks the lock, pulls out several files and moves to the desk.

She turns on the desk lamp, lays out the files and takes out a camera. She starts to take pictures. Inside are bills for a ship called "Ocean's Quest" and oceanographic charts of the Pacific Ocean near the Central American Coast. Alexa stiffens, turns toward the door and cups her ear. She tucks her camera away and flips off the light.

BAM! The door bursts open. Greg Grimm, dressed in a security uniform, gun drawn, charges in, followed by two more guards.

"Freeze!" Greg bellows.

Alexa hurls a small egg-shaped ball at the floor. It explodes with a blinding flash. Greg and the two guards are confused, but still open fire, shooting wildly. Alexa leaps about, avoiding their shots and throws another ball at the window. It sticks and starts to tick. Greg and the guards charge in, Alexa fights them off.

BOOM! The bomb explodes, the window shatters. Alexa heads for the window, and Greg tackles her.

"Help me! Get this... this freaky fool nailed down."

The Guards leap into the fray. Alexa kicks one away and throws Greg off of her, tossing him at the other guard. She turns toward the window, and Greg sticks out his foot, tripping Alexa. She tumbles out the window.

Greg and the guards get up and move to the window.

Greg laughs. "Ha, so much for that one. Let's head down to the street with a mop!"

Outside, Alexa plunges toward the ground below. She struggles to extend her wings, and finally does so. She flies off, arcing across the moon.

The next day, Alexa and Arthur sit in Arthur's lab; it's the very latest in high-tech science and research. All manner of computers, lasers etc. cover every one of the many tables. Stacks of big, thick books are scattered all over the room. Alexa sits on a stool and finishes putting a bandage on her bruised ribs. Arthur stands at his computer.

"How you feeling, kiddo?"

"I'll be fine. You should see the other guys!"

"I'm sure. So, let me tell you what I found."

At that moment, Katrina, a petite girl of thirteen with jet-black hair, and decked out to play, bounds into the room.

"Pop, are you done patching up Alexa from another of her stupid trips?"

"Katrina, darlin', yes, I am. But-"

"Good, then come play with me! I want to go to the beach."

"Bratina, beat it! We're-"

"Don't call me that! I'll tell mom. She said you're not allowed to call me that any more."

"Go, now, or I'll cut the heads off of all of your Barbies."

"You do, and I'll super glue them to the hood of your car!"

"If you're not out of here in two seconds, I'll post that video of you getting your baby bath in the kitchen sink on You Tube."

Katrina's jaw drops. She bolts for the door. "I'm going, I'm going!"

Arthur sighs. "Alexa, one of these days, she's going to call your bluff on that."

"Yeah, but 'til then, it'll keep her off my back. So, what you got for me?"

"I did some checking on Globe-Corp. They came out of nowhere a few years ago, to become a Fortune 500 firm. They've done a lot of work in disaster relief, particularly after tsunamis. And they helped in New Orleans."

"Well, that's pretty decent of them. They got any dirt under their nails on anything else?"

Arthur nods. "Oh yeah! Seems they've been buying up lots of the lands devastated by those waves and storms, developing them and re-selling them. They've made a fortune doing things like that."

"Ahh, sound like pretty bad boys, and girls. So, what's there interest in Nueva Libre?"

"Good question. What did they stand to gain by killing the Minister of Commerce? Did they want to stop our factory from being built?"

Alexa snaps her fingers. "Or, did he prevent them from exploiting the country?"

"I'll check them out, thoroughly; see what their interests in the area are."

Meanwhile, back in Kelly's office; the place is a mess, papers everywhere, furniture smashes and glass fragments litter the floor.

Kelly stands there, she looks furious, and Greg is at the door.

"So, you let her get away," Kelly says slowly.

"Sorry, Ma'am, but-"

"I don't care to hear your excuses! Anything missing?"

"We're not sure yet. After all, look at the condition-"

"And no pictures of her either? We've got more security than a Las Vegas Casino, and you didn't get a single picture!"

"She disabled the camera. Clearly, an expert cat burglar. She was wearing some sort of climbing gear or-"

Kelly rolls her eyes. "Are you truly as dumb as you look? A thief just happens to break into the high security floor the night after Doc' Mayhew and his 'Wonder Daughter' stop by for a visit!"

She slaps his face. Greg grinds his teeth.

"You think they had something to do with it? How could they know about this floor? It could just be a coincidence."

Kelly flips through the papers scattered about. "I don't believe in them! Anything found on the street below?"

"A few tattered papers. We got all of them before the cops arrived."

"Well, at least you managed to do one thing right! Now, here's what I want you to do, find out all you can about the Mayhews. Where they live, family, friends, what they're working on - everything. If they're responsible for this, I want them - dealt with."

Greg grins. "It'll be a pleasure."

At the same time, Alexa limps in to her lab.

"Oh, Alexa! Are you all right, sweetie? Perhaps some chicken soup would help," HEIDI says.

"Has my mother been re-programming you? It looks worse than it is, HEIDI. With my rapid metabolism, I'll be healed by tonight. I found some things for you to check on."

"You got it. Oh, I identified that man you sketched."

"Greg Grimm, Globe-Corp's Chief of Security," they both says.

HEIDI sighs. "I hate when you do that."

Alexa laughs. "Sorry. I happened to... run into him last night. I've got some pictures for you to review."

"You got it!"

A port swings open on the side of the computer. Alexa pulls out his camera. "Then open wide and say: ahhh."

"Ahhhhh."

Alexa hooks up the camera. "There you go. Also, check ship's registry for the 'Ocean's Quest'. I need the full skinny on it."

"Processing," HEIDI says, and then falls silent for a moment. "Hmmm, charts of the Pacific, all along the western coast of Central America. Bills for supplies for the 'Ocean's Quest', and some sort of chemical formula."

"Any idea what it's for?"

"Unknown. Given time, I may be able to extrapolate its function. Ah, here's the data on that ship. Currently doing deep sea research off the coast of Nueva Libre City."

Alexa sighs. "Ah-huh. Oh boy, looks like I'm going to rack up a lot more frequent flier miles."

"You going back there?"

"Got to, it's the only clue we've got at this point. I sure can't go back to their offices; they'll be on the lookout for me."

CHAPTER 2
SEARCHING FOR CLUES

The next day, in the clean open sky over the ocean a few clouds dot the horizon, and the Mayhew jet soars over the picturesque village of Aqua Grande Harbor on the shores of the Pacific. Modern ships mingle with ancient boats in the harbor.

Later, Alexa walks along the dock and studies the various ships. Finally, she comes to the "Ocean's Quest" and stops. A gangway leads up to the stern of the medium-sized research ship. Standing there, with her back to Alexa, is Linda Hart, tall and athletic, and decked out in shorts, t-shirt and flip-flops. She bends over and picks up an oxygen tank.

Behind Alexa, Steve Cutter, tall and lean, with a neatly trimmed beard walks up. "Ah-hem."

Alexa jumps in surprise and turns around. Linda straightens up and spins around.

"Darling!" Linda squeals.

She throws out her arms and dashes toward Alexa. She looks at her, totally surprised. Linda zips by her and embraces Steve. Alexa turns to look at them.

Linda breaks from her embrace and sees Alexa. "Oh. Hello. Can we help you?"

"Hi there; Alexa Mayhew, I'm doing an article about oceanographic research and wanted to speak to you."

She extends her hand to Linda. She smiles and shakes it.

"An article? That would be awesome! Why don't you come aboard? We've been doing some fascinating mapping of the mid ocean ridge and marine animal migratory patterns. Forget an article; I've got enough for a book."

Steve laughs. "Linda, calm down and take a breath. I'm Steve Cutter, her boyfriend and assistant."

"And I'm Linda Hart, Captain of the Ocean's Quest, best ocean-going research vessel there is!"

"You'll have to forgive her, Ms Mayhew. She's easily excited."

"Only about things I truly love and believe in! Protecting the natural world is my greatest passion in life."

Alexa nods. "Nothing wrong with that; sounds like you've been all over this area of the Pacific, I'd love to have a look at your ship."

Steve rubs his chin. "Mayhew, Mayhew... that name is familiar. Where have I... Wait! I know, isn't your company the one that's opening the new factory near here? Some little village just up the coast."

"Oh, why yes, we are. I'm as dedicated to it as much as you're dedicated to nature. It's going to-"

"Exploit the locals!" Linda snaps. "Oh, so you're that Mayhew. I'm sorry; I have nothing to say to an industrialist bent on polluting the environment and taking advantage of the poor."

Linda strides up the gangway without looking back.

Steve shrugs. "Sorry, lady; once Linda makes up her mind about something, that's it. Why don't you try National Geographic? I hear they'll talk to anyone."

Steve boards the boat. Alexa stands there, looks around and studies the dock area.

Much later, it's a dark and foggy night. A few small street lights and what little moonlight can pierce the clouds give the only light. Two armed security guards stand at the start of the dock. A shadowy figure swoops across the sky. Super Eagle drifts down out of the clouds and lands on the end of the dock. A board creaks. Alexa freezes. The guards chat together.

Alexa makes her way quickly and quietly to the gangway and boards the "Ocean's Quest". She moves along the deck to an open doorway, and enters. Inside is a small, efficient space. A desk with a lamp and numerous files sits in the center of the room. Pictures of endangered marine animals cover the walls, except for behind the desk. There a huge nautical chart with notations hangs.

Alexa closes the blinds and turns on the light. Quickly, she flips through the files. "Hmmm... all their supplies are coming through the village of Mariposa. Why is that name familiar?"

She looks at the nautical chart. Pulling out her camera, she takes a picture of it, and some of the files.

"Huh, they've been all over the place. Mapping the ocean ridge, eh? Why, what are they really up to? Why is Globe-Corp funding them?"

Outside, Steve and Linda approach the dock. They show their ID to the guards, and are waved through. Walking to the boat, hand in hand, they go aboard.

"This was great, Steve, just what I needed."

"Hey, you've been working hard, a night on the town is important once in a while."

Linda smiles. "True! So, you ready to tackle those humpbacks tomorrow."

Steve forces a smile on his face. "Sure. Love it. How about a-?"

"Night! I've got to check on some things on my office," Linda says, and bolts for her office door, leaving Steve standing there.

In Linda's office, Alexa continues to take pictures. She stiffens and turns toward the door. The handle turns. She backs away and looks around. Looking up, she bends her legs and shoots straight up to the ceiling.

The door opens and Linda enters. She crosses to the chart, picks up a notepad, and writes down some notes.

Above, Alexa clings to the ceiling with his talons. Her muscles strain and she sweats. Linda tears off her notes and stuffs them in her pocket. Turning, she heads for the door. Alexa breaths a sigh of relief. Steve pops in the door.

Linda jumps. "Steve! Gee, scare the snot out of me, why don't you? What up?"

"I just remembered something. If we're heading out tomorrow, we'll need those new supplies. Did you check on them today?"

Alexa grits her teeth as she struggles to maintain her grip.

"Yeah, I took care of them. They arrived this afternoon."

Steve smiles. "Oh, thank goodness! You know, Linda, if you want, I'll take care of the supplies from now on. After all, you've got enough on your plate. Why be bothered with-?"

"Steve, it's no bother. When you're trusting your life to your equipment, you want to make sure it's the best!"

"Okay, you're call."

"Come on, let's turn in. I feel like I'm going to drop right here!"

Alexa looks down at them and mouths: "Me too!"

Linda nods toward her desk. "And, remind me to talk to the crew again tomorrow about leaving lights on. It drains the batteries!"

Linda switches off the light, and they exit. Alexa releases her feet, swings down so she's dangling from her hands and drops silently to the floor. She rubs her sore arms and legs, and moves to the door.

Alexa moves down the gangway. The guards talk between themselves. She heads for the end of the dock, takes wing and flies off into the moonlit sky.

The next day, on Eagle Island, the harbor is busy with fishing boats heading out for the first catch of the day. Greg Grimm moves about the area, talks to lots of people, and makes some notes.

Later, Greg stands near the stone jetty and talks on his cellphone to Kelly, as she sits at the desk in her office.

"So, Arthur is quite the scientific geniuses, eh?"

Greg nods. "Yeah, everyone in town calls Arthur a regular 'Dr. Quest', whatever that means."

"Greg, weren't you ever a kid? You ever watch Saturday morning cartoons?"

"Ahh..."

"Never mind! What about Alexa, where is she and what's her story?"

"Ah, now that's where things get interesting. She was hospitalized a couple years back and almost died. The scuttlebutt here is that her dad used her as a human guinea pig, and something went way wrong!"

"But, she lived! So, who gives a flying flip? What is she up to right now, you moron?"

"I don't know. She flew out of here yesterday and-"

Kelly jumps to her feet. "What? You blithering idiot! Find her. Tear that place-"

"Miss Delaney, calm yourself, I'm way ahead of you. I slipped a mechanic at the airport a few bucks, and he gave me the full 411. Alexa took the family jet back to Neuva Libre."

Kelly pounds her desk. "What? You get on the next flight down there at once! I'll call Miss Hart and see if she's found out about her connection to us."

"You got it."

"Wait, what about her family? Alexa's mother living? Any siblings?"

"Family? Ah, yeah. Her mom's quite the local artist, and she's got a younger sister."

Kelly grins and sits down. "Excellent. If Alexa learns too much, we know just where to... 'squeeze' to keep her in line."

Meanwhile, in the town of Mariposa, a quaint mountain village with stone buildings and cobblestone streets, a farmers' market is in full swing in the town's center. Alexa mills about, pretending to look at the produce, but really watching the armed men standing guard on the rooftops of the surrounding buildings.

"Now I remember this place. That minister Pop and I met with said it was a rebel stronghold. So, why is Globe-Corp routing supplies for Miss Hart's research ship through here?"

Alexa travels around the town, talking with many people. From the shadows, armed men watch her, and a little girl watches them. Later that evening, in a small, simple cafe with umbrella-covered tables, Alexa sits at a table and eats dinner. Half a dozen other people sit at other tables and eat. Around her, men move in the shadows. The other people start to get up and walk away, one or two at a time.

Alexa's eyes dart back and forth as she notices that she's slowly becoming alone. She stands and puts some money on the table, then slips her hand in her pocket. A dozen men leap out and surround her, all aiming their weapons at her.

A short, squat fellow steps forward. "Don't move, Senorita, we have orders to deliver you to El Supremo."

Alexa's brow wrinkles. "The Almighty? You're taking me to meet God? That'll be quite a trick. I was really rather hoping to delay that for about eighty years or so."

The man grins, showing his yellow and chipped teeth. "Our boss has a bit of a god complex. Still, her money is as green as anyone else's, so we don't mind humoring her."

"If it's a question of money, I'll match whatever she's paying you. There's no reason we can't-"

"I don't think so, Senorita. It's bad for business to betray an employer. Now, come along quietly, and we won't hurt you - too much."

"Sorry, must dash," Alexa says as she pulls a small egg-shaped object out of her pocket and hurls it to the ground.

FOOSH! A cloud of white envelopes the entire cafe. Alexa leaps straight up into the air and latches onto the wall of the building. She climbs up onto the roof and takes off. The men cough and hack and rush the table. A moment later, the smoke clears; the leader is at the bottom of a huge pile of men, all of them pounding on him.

"Get off me, you loco burros! Spread out, look everywhere."

They un-pile from him, mumbling their apologies, and scan the area.

Another man points up at the rooftop. "There she goes!"

"After her! A new rifle to the man who brings me her eyeballs."

The men take off after Alexa. BANG, POP! They open fire at her. Alexa leaps from building to building, trying to lose them. Chunks of brickwork crack and fly away as the bullets hit the building around her. She finally comes to a dead end street; a narrow cobblestone road, lined with old and crumbling buildings. She bounds along the rooftops. The rebels race along the road firing at her as she leaps and jumps.

Alexa leaps across the street, but a stray shot catches her in the shoulder. She slams into the side of the building she was trying to jump to, reaches up and snags the top edge. She hangs there as the men race into the dead end street.

"Where is she, did anyone see where she went? Spread out, search!" the leader shouts.

The men look around. The leader stands almost directly under Alexa. She grimaces in pain and clings desperately to the crumbling building facade. A drop of blood falls from her wounded shoulder and lands right next to the man. The stone Alexa is gripping starts to give way. She tries to grab another with her wounded arm, but can't get a good hold on it.

Anna, a small waif of a girl in a simple dress steps out of a doorway. She points off down a narrow alley. "Sir, sir, I saw an American run down that way!"

The leader spins to face her. "Good girl! This way, men! Keep your eyes open and weapons ready. We want her alive, but wounded it okay."

He leads his men off down the alley. Anna waits until they're gone, and then looks up at Alexa. She gestures for her to come down. Alexa chews his lip, uncertainty written on her face. But, she's clearly exhausted.

She lets go and crumbles to the ground. Anna races to her side and helps her to her feet. She heads her into a rundown building.

Inside is a bleak, desolate open space. A few mean pieces of furniture and an oil lamp are the only things in it. Alexa sits with her back against the wall, her shirt off, and Anna bandages her wounded shoulder.

"I sorry, miss, but this the best I know how to do."

Alexa smiles at her. "It's all right, darlin', you've done fine. But, why? Why are you helping me? You don't even know me!"

Anna laughs. "Si, Senorita, I do. You, you and your papa, you come to my village for your... ah, your work place."

Alexa chews her lip as she tries to think. "Ah, you mean our new factory! Oh, so, you come from Punta Gorda. But, what are you doing here?"

Anna hangs her head. "My... my papa. He... he join the rebels when... when my mama went to Heaven."

Alexa pats her head. "I'm so sorry for your loss..."

"Anna. It is all right. I... I just miss my gramma and grampa."

"Well, you helped me, Anna, and I will help you. If you like, I'll take you back to them."

Anna's face lights up with joy. "You will! Oh, thank you."

Alexa gets to her feet and moves to the window. She tilts her head, listening. From outside come the sounds of running feet. She turns to Anna. "It's a promise! What about your papa, will he come with us?"

Anna shakes her head. "No, Miss, he will never leave. He say... he say the company woman promised them gold if they carry their boxes through the mountains."

"Ah, so that's what Globe-Corp wanted; a way to get their supplies to Miss Hart without being inspected. I bet that's why they wanted the minister dead; he was pushing for tighter border security. Is there another way out of here? I think those soldiers are still searching for me."

Anna heads for a backdoor. "Si, come, we go this way, through the store room."

They move through the door and enter a dark, dank room filled with stacks and stacks of huge crates. All of them have the Globe-Corp logo on them. Anna leads Alexa down the aisles between the crates, heading for a heavy wooden door. Alexa stops and stares at the crates.

"What the-? Ah, here's the proof, Globe-Corp's supplies! If we can get this to the authorities, it'll prove that they're behind the rebels."

"Que? Oh, the boxes. Si, the American men bring guns and bullets, and tell the men where to go."

Alexa grinds his teeth. "Yeah, well I'd like to tell them where to go!"

Anna gets a questioning look to her face. "Where?"

"Ahhh... home to their mommies! They all deserve a good spanking."

Anna giggles and heads for the door. Alexa smiles, then stiffens.

"You funny, Senorita."

"Anna, get away from the door!"

BOOM! A loud explosion rocks the building. Dust and debris falls from the ceiling. The door blasts inward, knocking Anna to the floor. Alexa races to her side. With a mighty heave, she tosses the door aside. Alexa gathers Anna into her arms and races out the door.

Outside is a small open area surrounded by low, crumbling buildings.

The sky is ablaze with explosions. Rebels race about, firing into the air. Army Helicopters hover overhead and fire cannons and rockets at the buildings. Alexa looks over the area and bolts for a small building. Gunfire follows her, and she ducks and weaves to avoid getting hit. She lays Anna down, turns and assesses the situation.

BOOM! KA-BOOM! The buildings around her are rocked by explosions. The one she and Anna came out of erupts into a huge fireball, debris flies everywhere. Alexa throws herself down to protect Anna as the battle continues to rage on around them.

The next morning, the "Ocean's Quest" moves through the gentle surf of the Pacific under the clear, blue sky, heading toward port. Several deckhands move about the ship. Linda, Greg and Steve stand at the bow; Greg seems to be looking over the railing at something.

"Ah, is there anything better than this?" Linda asks. "Clean air, open skies, the rolling ocean; this is all that's best in life! Don't you agree?"

Greg straightens up and turns to Linda, he is clearly seasick. "Oh yes, delightful."

Steve grins. "You're looking a little green around the gills there, fella. Guess boating isn't your strong suit."

Linda gives him a cold stare. "We're very grateful to all that Globe-Corp has done in support of our research. So, now that you've seen us in action, I hope you'll give Miss Delaney a favorable report."

Silvana bends toward the phone. "Is there any way we can send the police or a search party to-?"

"No, I'm afraid not. The army is swarming all over that area. You try to snoop around in there, you'll get arrested, or worse! Have you tried her cellphone?"

"Yes. Nothing. But, I figured she was just out of range. Now..." Arthur says, his voice trailing off.

"My condolences. If I hear anything, I'll let you know at once. And please, if you hear from him, let me know."

Silvana wipes a tear from her cheek. "Of course. And thank you, Miss Delaney, for all your help."

Arthur hangs up the phone. He moves to Silvana and Katrina and embraces them both. "Let's not jump to any conclusions here. Until we know for certain, we-"

Katrina breaks away from her parents. "The big dope! Why'd she have to go and get herself killed?"

She bolts from the room, crying.

Meanwhile, Kelly talks on the phone. "Yes, general, it's confirmed; Alexa Mayhew is one of the rebel leaders. I'll fax you her picture today. She was last seen in Mariposa, and should be shot on sight!"

Kelly hangs up and sits back in her chair, an evil grin on her face.

At the same time, on a winding dirt road that meanders through the thick trees of the countryside, a horse-drawn wagon moves slowly along the road as rain pours down and thunder and lightning fills the sky. Alexa and Anna sit in the back. Anna shivers and rubs her hands together. Alexa tries her best to protect Anna from the driving rain. In the distance, headlights can be seen.

"Military trucks are following us!" Anna says.

"Are you sure?"

"Si, Senorita, I have seen many of them chasing mi padre and his... friends."

"I hope we can stay ahead of them." She pulls a tattered coat from her pack and hands it to Anna. "Here, take this. Maybe you can stay warm and get some rest."

"Gracia. Oh, but what about you?"

"The cold doesn't bother me."

Anna covers herself as best she can, lies down and tries to sleep. Alexa looks off into the stormy sky, and watches the distant headlights. Slowly, the scene changes to her father's lab as Alexa remembers another stormy night from long ago. Out the window can be seen a dark and stormy night. Alexa, about ten years old, enters.

"Mom, Pop, you here? The storm's really scaring me. Can I get another of those tranquilizers?"

She looks around the room. On a bench sits a small beaker of red liquid. Its label reads: "TRAN".

"Pop! Where are-? Oh, there's one."

She sees the beaker, picks it up and drinks it. She heads for the door. Suddenly, she doubles over in pain, and staggers from the room. She makes her way into the dimly lit living room. Flashes of lightning can be seen through the windows.

"Arrrrgggggg! OW! Mom, Pop, help me!"

She stumbles out the door and into the beautifully landscaped yard. The back of the yard slopes up toward a distant hill. The storm rages, wind, rain, thunder and lightning; Alexa staggers through the yard and up the hill.

"Mom! Pop! King, are you there?"

A bald eagle swoops down and lands on a nearby branch. Alexa drops to the ground and looks up at the eagle.

"King, help me. Go get-"

CRACK! A bolt of lightning engulfs Alexa and King. Silence. King flies off. Alexa lies on the ground.

The next morning, Alexa lies in her bed. Arthur and Silvana hover over her. Silvana is very pregnant. Alexa groans and slowly opens her eyes.

"Alexa, can you hear me?" Silvana asks.

"Sweetie, talk to us!"

Alexa sits up a little. "I'm... hungry."

Silvana wipes a tear from her eye. "That's the best thing I've ever heard! I'll go fix you something."

She races out, walking as fast as she can. Arthur closes the door and turns to Alexa.

"Alexa, did you drink the transformation formula? It was gone when I went to the lab this morning."

"Trans-? I thought it was a tranquilizer. I didn't know-"

"It's okay; it's not your fault. It was mine; I never should have left it out! Are you feeling okay?"

"Sure. I-"

Alexa looks over Arthur's shoulder and out the window. Offshore, a sailboat moves across the horizon. Alexa's eye zooms in on the boat, and she sees four people enjoying a day of sailing.

"Pop, I can see the Boydens and their kids out sailing!"

Arthur spins around and looks out the window, then turns back to Alexa. "Oh - my - God. It worked!"

"What worked? What are you talking about?"

"I've been experimenting with an extract that would give people the strength of an eagle."

"So, I'm going to turn into an eagle? Cool! Oh, I can't wait to tell mom."

"No, Alexa, you mustn't say a word to her! Not in her... condition. And no, you're not going to turn into an eagle."

Alexa frowns. "Awwwww, crude. But, okay, I won't say a word to her."

The scene returns to the present, an asphalt road, rather narrow with a few broken street lights and a cracked sidewalk head into the city of Aqua Grande. Alexa stands on the sidewalk, Anna on her back, sound asleep. Alexa waves to the horse-drawn cart owner as he moves off down the road.

"We made it, Darlin', we're here. Now, all we have to-"

She sees a wanted poster on a nearby tree; it has her picture on it, and a reward of $250,000. Anna lifts her head from her shoulder.

"What, what we do? Is all okay?"

Alexa swallows hard. "Yes! Yes, everything's fine. I just... need to... figure out the best way to... the hotel."

Alexa looks around, concerned written across her face. Slowly, she makes her way into town. Alexa and Anna make there way down dark alleys and hide in shadowy doorways. Police and soldiers race about, searching for them.

Eventually, they come to a hotel and enter. A moment later, they step into a small, simple room, yet very elegant and tidy with a bed, dresser, table and a couple of chairs. Alexa closes and locks the door, then plops Anna on the bed. Alexa moves to the window and cautiously peeks out. Closing the drapes, she pulls a suitcase out from under the bed and opens it.

"Senorita, I mean, Alexa, I so hungry. Have we any food?"

Alexa roots around in her bag and pulls out a pack of energy bars. "Here you go, darlin', these'll keep you going."

Anna takes them and tears open the bag, feasting on them. "Oh, these are good! Alexa, can I ask you question? How is it you are all better? I never see anyone heal so fast."

"Oh, that's a long story. Let's just say, my dad gave me a super chocolate shake that made me stronger."

"What is chocolate?"

Alexa looks shocked. "You've never had chocolate? Oh, darlin', we got to get you fixed up. We'll work on that as soon as we get out of here. Okay?"

"Si."

Alexa pulls out a small device that looks like a portable DVD player. Switching it on, she punches a series of buttons. The screen is full of snow and static. "Come on, Dad, be there!"

In Alexa's lab, Arthur piles some papers on top of a stack of books, and then puts them away on a shelf. The sound of crying is heard around him.

"HEIDI, try to control yourself. We still don't know what's happened to her. She could be all right."

"I am okay, and I am sure she is fine. I calculate better than a ninety-seven percent probability that she survived the government attack. I am concerned about the bounty the government has put on her head."

Arthur nods. "Yes, so am I. How on earth did they come to think she was a rebel leader?"

BEEP-BEEP!

"Arthur, it is Alexa's CommUnit!"

Arthur drops everything - right on his foot! "Ow-ow-ow!"

He hops about, clutching his foot. Heidi giggles. A small flat screen rises from a computer panel. It switches on, static and snow appear for a moment, and then Alexa's face appears. Arthur hops over to the screen, smiling at Alexa.

"Pop, what's up, you inventing a new dance?"

"Oh, hardy-har-har. Sweetie, you don't know how glad I am to see you!"

"You don't how glad I feel to be seen. We've gone through... heck getting back here."

"We?" Arthur asks.

"Bio-scan indicates a female juvenile is in his room," Heidi says.

Anna steps into view. "Is she talking about me?"

Arthur gasps. "What the-? Alexa, you want to explain?"

"Long story, Pop. She helped me, and I'm going to help her."

Arthur nods. "You got it! Now, let's get you out of there."

Alexa plugs her camera into the transmitter and then holds up a small mechanical device.

"No, I can't leave. Take a look at these pictures and check this out. HEIDI, scan it and see if you can figure out what it is. Globe-Corp is up to something down here, and it's big! They wouldn't fund the rebels unless it meant a major score for them."

A series of beeps and chirps come from HEIDI as she scans the device and downloads the picture. Arthur flips through the pictures on a nearby screen.

"Alexa, what does that chart show?"

"It was on the 'Ocean's Quest'. It's got the coordinates of all the places they've been going."

"Oh my! Alexa, Arthur, that device is a nuclear trigger," HEIDI says.

"What?" they both say.

Arthur frowns. "That fits! Alexa, that ship has been visiting key spots around the Pacific Plate."

Anna shakes her head. "Plate? Are they eating something?"

"You could say that, Anna. If it's what I think, they're going to be 'eating' a good portion of South America!"

Arthur nods. "A series of nukes planted at those locations, and detonated together would cause a massive tsunami. It would destroy most of the west coast of the continent!"

Anna gasps. "My home! Gramma, grampa!"

Alexa pats her arm. "Don't worry, darlin', we won't let that happen. Pop, have my boat sent down here."

"Alexa, do you think that's wise? We've been monitoring the government radio traffic; the troops have orders to shoot you on sight!"

"Madre de Dios!" Anna cries.

"Anna, no matter what, you'll be okay. Pop, I've got to stop them!"

"Alexa, as that trigger is clearly from a damaged nuclear weapon, is there anything to be concerned about? The bombs were all destroyed in the government raid, were not they?" HEIDI asks.

"We can't know that for certain. So, I'm going to check them out!"

Arthur nods. "All right; I'll ship your boat to the factory site. We can hide it in among the crates of machine parts."

"Good, we'll head there immediately. Anna, we're going to your home."

Anna's eyes light up. "That wonderful! Oh, but, will you be safe?"

"I'll be fine. Pop, I'll be in touch as soon as I can. Tell mom and "Bratina" I'm fine."

Arthur laughs. "I'll tell them."

Alexa switches off the CommUnit and puts it away. She stiffens, spins around and moves to the door.

Out in the hallway, Greg leads a squad of government troops, all armed with automatic weapons toward Alexa's room. Slowly, they move in from all sides.

Alexa stands with her ear pressed against the door. She steps back, spins around and moves to her bag. She roots around in it and pulls out a small device. It looks like a small tube with an eagle's talon at each end.

"We need to leave, now! And through the door."

She throws open the window. Aiming the device at the wall next to the door, she fires it. A talon, trailing a stout cable, shoots out of one end and embeds itself in the wall. She turns and shoots the other talon out the window. It trails a cable across to the next building. Holding the device, she gestures to Anna.

"Come on, darlin', we're out of here!"

"Out the window?"

BANG! POW! Gunfire erupts outside the door. Bullets tear through the door. Anna rushes to her.

"Madre di Dios!"

She pulls Anna up onto her back and steps up to the window. "Pop, I hope this gizmo works."

BAM! The door flies off its hinges as the troops break it down. They rush into the room, guns blazing. Alexa squeezes the device, a rocket fires and it carries them out the window; they race across the open space between the hotel and an adjoining building. Soldiers appear at the window, they open fire at them. Alexa swings and sways wildly, trying to avoid their shots.

Greg stands behind the soldiers and watches as they fire out the window, a smug little smile on his face. He notices the cable, reaches up and plucks it. Whipping out a knife, with one deft slice, he cuts the cable.

"Bon Voyage, Alexa Mayhew. Watch that first step, it's a long one."

The end of the cable sails out the window. Alexa and Anna plunge earthward. The soldiers turn to Greg. He puts his knife away and wipes his hands.

"So, shall we go down and mop up?"

He laughs and leads them out the door.

Meanwhile, in an apartment in the adjoining building, a cleaning woman, short and a bit frumpy stands in the middle of the room and wipes the sweat from her brow.

"Ah, muy bueno!"

CRASH! The window shatters as Alexa, with Anna on her back, swings through the window and deftly makes a landing. Anna flies off her back, slams into the woman and the two of them tumble to the floor. Alexa stands up, races over to them and scoops Anna up.

"So sorry, can't stay, must dash. Lovely place." She looks around. "Oh, ah, sorry about the window."

She pulls a wad of cash from her pocket and stuffs it in the cleaning woman's hand; and then carries Anna to the door and they leave. The woman gets to her feet, looks around and heaves a big sigh.

Meanwhile, Linda stands at her desk and looks at her chart as she talks on the phone to Kelly. "Yes, I know the area you mean. But, Miss Delaney, do you really think we need to move things up?"

Kelly sits at her desk. "Absolutely! All that rebel activity has caused a lot of bad press. Our project will distract everyone from that."

Linda smiles. "True, it will do that! Okay, we'll advance our timetable twenty-four hours. Give us one more day, and we'll make headlines around the world!"

Kelly grins. "Excellent!"

Out on a quiet narrow street there are a few beaten and battered cars parked here and there. Alexa and Anna crouch near a car as Alexa works to pick the lock.

"Alexa, this is not right! This is stealing!"

"Yes, it is, but we have no choice. Those men seek to kill us! We must get to Punta Gorda. So, we need a car."

She pops the door open and they get in. Down the street come several soldiers. Alexa sees them approaching the in the rearview mirror. She works as fast as she can to hotwire the car. The soldiers get closer. The engine starts and Alexa races away. The soldiers take aim and fire, shooting out the rear window.

"Ahhhhh! They shooting!" Ana cries.

"Look on the bright side, now we've got air conditioning! Buckle up; it's going to be a bumpy ride."

She races off down the street and the soldiers continue to fire. Soon she is driving down a narrow, dirt road in the countryside. As time passes, night falls, and Anna sleeps in the backseat. Alexa checks her map and reads the road signs as she passes one that says Punta Gorda is five kilometers away.

Meanwhile, out in the open ocean, the moon hangs low in the sky, backlighting the "Ocean's Quest" as it sits at anchor, near a buoy. Linda and Steve stand on the deck as men in scuba gear move a crates over the side.

"Will they be able to get it into position in time?" Linda asks.

Steve nods. "Leave it to me, Linda. Everything will be ready by dawn. Then we just head back to port."

"I knew I could count on you, darling!"

The next morning, the sun rises, and illuminates a huge construction site. Buildings are half built, power lines partially strung along the road, equipment and crates are everywhere. Nearby, down the steep slope of a hill, is the small harbor of Punta

Gorda. Alexa's car sits off to the side, under a tree. She works to open a crate. Anna sits on the hood of the car and yawns.

"So, where do your grandparents live?"

"Near the harbor, a cottage on the north shore."

"Wonderful! I'll drop you there on my way out to sea."

"Will you be okay? The soldiers are everywhere!"

"Don't worry about me. We'll get you home and then I'll handle the bad guys! Ah, here we go."

THUMP! The crate falls open to reveal her sleek, futuristic super speedboat. Anna hops off the hood and crosses to it.

"Ohhhh, pretty!"

Alexa lifts Anne into it, then jumps and spins around. "Ahh... I think we need to go!"

She hops in, starts it and puts it in gear.

"But, this is boat, and we're on land," Anna says.

"Not to worry, this baby comes fully loaded!"

ZOOM! The boat races along the dirt road, down the hill and heads for the harbor. A moment later, three army jeeps burst from the trees, slam on their breaks and kick up dust as them come to a stop around the car. Soldiers swarm out to check the area. One sees the boat off in the distance, shouts and points. They pile back into the jeeps and race after the boat.

At the bottom of the hill sits the quaint little harbor dotted with small fishing boats. People move about the harbor, preparing the boats for the day's fishing. Alexa's boat roars down the hill, shoots across a dock and lands in the water. She races across the harbor.

Anna throws up her arms. "Wwhhheeeeeee! This fun."

Alexa look over her shoulder and sees the jeeps racing down the dock. The first slams on his breaks and stops at the end. The next stops and taps the first, pushing it closer to the edge. The third stops, taps the second, which taps the first. Its wheels go over the edge, and it tumbles into the water.

Alexa laughs. "Yes, darlin', it's a load of laughs."

Alexa races around the harbor and moves up the coastline. Anna points to a small cottage sitting nestled back among a cluster of trees. Alexa pulls into shore and cuts the engine. She pulls the boat ashore and then helps Anna to the beach. Alexa gets down on one knee and smiles at her.

She hugs Alexa. "Gracia, Alexa, how can I ever thank you?"

"Grow up to be as smart as you can, and never let anyone put you down! Tell your grandparents to bring you to the factory when it's done. I'll see that they get jobs, and you get an education. Now, I must go. Will you be okay?"

The door of the cottage opens. An elderly couple steps out. Anna and Alexa turn to look at them.

Anna smiles. "Si, there they are!"

"Go to them."

Anna races up the beach toward the cottage. The couple recognizes her and cries out in joy. They embrace. Alexa pushes the boat back into the water, hops in and races off. Three military speedboats come around the coastline and give chase. They open fire. BOOM BAM BANG! Bullets and bombs explode around her. She swerves and arcs across the water. Smoke starts to spew out of the back of her boat. It envelopes the others and two get disoriented. BOOM! They crash into each other.

The third boat continues to fire, and closes in on Alexa. Machine gun fire slices across her port side. She throws a switch. ZZZAAPPPP! Lightning bolts dance between her boat and the other one. POP BANG! The other boat's motor and electrical system short out. They're dead in the water. Alexa races off, even as they continue to shoot at her. She ducks.

CHAPTER 4
THE FIGHT TO STOP THEM!

Later, out on the open ocean, Alexa stands at the bow and scans the area. She holds a GPS locator. Near the horizon floats a buoy.

"Nearly there. I should go to... there, near that buoy."

She moves back to the wheel, switches on the engine and moves the boat close to the buoy. Cutting the engine, she grabs a device and switches on the communicator.

Back in Alexa's lab, Arthur alternates between studying a series of satellite images of the Pacific Ridge and a print out of a complex chemical formula. BEEP BEEP!

"Arthur, it is Alexa!" HEIDI says.

Arthur turns, sending all the paperwork flying off the table. "Dagnabit! Oh, put her on."

The CommUnit springs to life; Alexa's face appears on the screen.

"Pop, HEIDI, I've located the first of the bombs."

The side of the buoy is open, all manner of wires and electronics hang out of it, and are strewn across the deck. Alexa studies them with her scanner.

Arthur smiles as he looks at the screen. "Excellent! Give us a SIT REP; think you can disarm it?"

"Well, the situation report is this: very simple arming mechanism, and the timer hasn't been set. I can 'pluck this chicken' in two shakes!"

"Fine, do so, and we'll fill you in on what we've found."

Alexa studies the components and begins to snip wires, disconnect devices and in general take things apart. "Okay, what you got, Pop?"

"Well, I–"

"Excuse me! Should not it be ladies first?" HEIDI snaps.

"Your pardon, HEIDI, go right ahead."

"Thank you. Alexa, I worked out that chemical formula. It is designed to remove C-O-two from the atmosphere, and thus ease the effects of Global Warming."

"It does? Interesting. If Globe-Corp has invented that, why cause a tsunami?" Alexa wonders.

"I can answer that," Arthur says. "The formula is extremely complex, and expensive! By causing a massive tidal wave, Globe-Corp stands to make a fortune. Plus, the bombs won't just cause a tsunami."

Alexa stops working and turns to look at the screen. A digital display resets to read sixty seconds and starts to count down.

"Huh? Why, what else could they be plan–? Oops. Ah, keep talking, Pop; I've got a... matter to attend to here."

Alexa works feverishly, desperately trying to disarm the device. Meanwhile, Arthur, totally oblivious to Alexa's peril, casually carries on.

"I've analyzed the locations of the bombs. Not only will their detonation cause a huge tidal wave, they will release massive amounts of lava, thus increasing the El Nino effect. As a result, Global Warming will be accelerated."

Alexa sweats, unsure which wire to cut.

"The blue one, Alexa, it is always the blue one," HEIDI says.

Alexa cuts the blue wire, the timer stops. "Whewww. Thanks, HEIDI. Ah, of course! Global Warming gets worse, the world cries out for a solution, and in steps Globe-Corp with just that."

Arthur nods. "Yes, an incredibly expensive solution, which the governments of the world will happily fork over all the money Globe-Corp asks for."

TEEK-TEEK-TEEK! The buoy starts to give off a series of sounds.

"Alexa, get out of there - now!" HEIDI says.

"Why, what's the matter? I thought I disarmed it!"

"You have, but you also tripped a warning beacon."

Alexa grabs a pair of wire cutters and starts yanking wires. "All right, I'll soon deal with that!"

"No, do not bother. The mechanism is buried deep within the buoy. Long before you could hope to reach it, the people who set it will find you."

"Alexa, I suggest you scram, and quickly!" Arthur says. "Make for port. Once there, call us back and we'll find another way to stop them."

Alexa kicks the components and wires overboard, and starts the engine. "I'm out of here!"

Back in Aqua Grande Harbor, the "Ocean's Quest" sits moored at the dock. The crew mills about on the deck. Linda and Steve walk up the dock toward the shore and enter a small warehouse that overhangs the harbor.

A few minutes later, in a small cramped room piled high with boxes with a single bare bulb providing the only light, a laptop sits atop a box. A warning message flashing on its screen, and a figure, seen only in shadows sits and starts typing.

In Punta Gorda, Greg and several soldiers search the area. His phone beeps. Pulling it from his waist, he sees that he's got a text message. He reads it.

"Oh, crap!"

He dials on his phone. Kelly, in her office, answers her phone.

"Oh, crap! Are you sure?"

"Just got it a moment ago. You know what this means, don't you?"

"Of course I do, idiot! She's figured it out, and she's outsmarted you again! You get back there, now. I'm going to go get us some insurance."

Greg's brow wrinkles. "Insurance?"

"Yes, I'll pay a visit to the family; see how mom, dad, and little sis' are doing."

"Excellent! Think they'll be a problem?"

Kelly opens the drawer of her desk. Inside is a pistol. "No, when Smith and Wesson talk, people listen."

She and Greg hang up. Greg hops into a jeep. He gestures for the soldiers to join him. They get in and race off, leaving a cloud of dust.

Back in Aqua Grande, outside the warehouse, Steve stands and talks on the phone. Linda comes out of the building.

"Steve, it's lunchtime. Send the crew off to eat; we've got a big day ahead of us."

"You got it. You coming?"

"No, got some paperwork to finish. Bring me back a veggie burger."

"You got it again. See ya!"

Steve gives her a small hug and a peck on the cheek. She heads back inside and he walks around the side of the building and out onto the dock.

At the same time, Alexa maneuvers her boat into the harbor's entrance. Off in the distance, she sees the crew of the "Ocean's Quest" leaving the boat and heading up the dock. Slowly, she approaches the dock, and sees the nearby warehouse. A crate with the Globe-Corp logo sits outside the back door. She ties up the boat, and then leaps up onto the deck of the warehouse.

Inside, in the neat and efficient office, Linda sits at the desk and makes notes on a pad of paper. THUMP! A sound comes from outside. She gives a little jump, stands and heads out the door.

Out in the main part of the warehouse, Alexa forces a crate open and looks inside. Explosives and detonators are there. She lets out a long whistle. The door of the warehouse opens, Linda comes out.

"What the-? What are you doing here?"

Alexa drops the lid. It slides off and Linda sees the contents.

"Oh - my - God! What are you doing?"

Alexa looks surprised. "Me? That's what I was going to ask you? Look at the crate; it's addressed to you!"

Linda steps closer. "Wha-? But I- This is supposed to be equipment for marine research!"

Steve and four thugs step around the corner.

"Oops, looks like someone opened her present before Christmas," Steve says, a grin on his face.

Linda looks confused. "Darling, what's the meaning of all-?"

"Oh, drop the mushy stuff, girlie, this is man's business!"

"What?"

Alexa sighs. "I think what 'Neanderthal Nick' is trying to say, is that his love for you was all a sham, part of Globe-Corp's plan to destroy most of the country."

Steve bows. "Thank you, thank you. Yes, quite the performance, wasn't it? A stud like me, with such a loser geek as her. Who'd have believed it?"

"Yes, quite the stretch. I'd expect her to have better taste!"

Steve feigns being shot in the heart. "Oh, cut down by that rapier-like wit of yours. I take it you're the one responsible for one of our nukes going off-line?"

Alexa bows to him. "Guilty as charged. So, looks like you're out of a job. Now, why not just give up, and turn yourselves over to the authorities?"

Steve and the thugs laugh.

"What, you think you've stopped us? No, we're heading out right now to repair it. The detonations will go off as planned. Thanks to Linda sending the crew away, we won't have to kill all of them, just you two."

"What?" Linda asks.

Alexa flips the crate lid up with one hand. It slams into Steve and the thugs, and they tumble backwards. Alexa grabs Linda and dashes into Linda's office. Alexa locks the door and rushes into her office and grabs the phone. Pounding comes from the outside and the door shakes.

"Linda, company's here. I suggest we don't let them in. I think we should take it on the lam!"

Linda drops the phone. "Line's dead!"

"I hope that's not an omen of things to come. Now, let's go!"

SMASH! The window shatters as a rock hurtles through it. Linda dashes out the other door and down the hall.

"Come no, I've got an idea."

Alexa follows. "Ah, my kind of woman!"

Linda dashes in the store room, followed by Alexa. She sees the laptop and picks it up.

"What's this?" Linda asks.

Alexa looks at the screen. "I'd say it's Steve's. Probably how he knew I'd deactivated one of the nukes."

CRASH! The sound of glass and wood breaking comes from the hall.

"Darn those Jehovah's Witnesses, they never take no for an answer. Ah, Linda, you said something about an idea!"

"Oh, right. Here, help me move this crate."

Linda grabs a crate and tries to move it, but can barely budge it. Alexa closes the door and goes to help her. With one shove, the crate moves to reveal a trap door, and is up against the door. Linda opens the door, the harbor water is below. BAM! The door rattles, but doesn't open. The crate shifts a bit.

Alexa gestures down the opening. "Age before beauty!"

Linda jumps. SPLASH! Alexa grabs a gasoline can, dumps it over the crates and strikes a match. WHOOSH! The place goes up in flames. She jumps. SPLASH! Alexa and Linda bob to the surface. She leads Linda toward her boat, but sees a thug on it. They stop and tread water. Steve and three thugs bolt out the back door of the warehouse, black smoke billows after them.

"Get out, get back, the whole building is going up!" Steve cries.

42

Flames leap from the warehouse roof. Alexa looks up. The floor above them starts to creak and groan as the board warp and crack. She looks at Linda.

"You any good at holding your breath?"

Linda looks at her as if to say: are you serious? They dive under. Steve and his four thugs move away from the building. The flames grow and the building starts to collapse into the water. Alexa's boat, some flaming debris on its side, starts to drift away.

"Hey, the boat!" one of the thugs says.

Steve snorts. "Let it go. They won't be needing it. As soon as the fuel catches, up it'll go. Now, come on, we've got a schedule to keep!"

Steve leads them to the "Ocean's Quest". They untie the boat and take off, leaving the harbor and making for the open ocean. Alexa and Linda surface next to her boat and climb aboard. She kicks the burning debris overboard, and Linda bleeds from a wound to her head.

"Well, that was fun," Alexa says.

"What in the world is going on here? I thought Globe-Corp was helping me with my research! But, that was just a cover, wasn't it?"

"Yes, I'm afraid so."

"What's their plan, and how do we stop them?"

"We don't! I'll handle them. You're hurt. You stay here and-"

Linda shakes her head. "I don't think so! I don't know what they're up to, but I'm going to help."

"Linda, be reasonable."

"Alexa, think about it. How are your navigating skills? You an expert diver? How are you going to get down there to disarm those nukes?"

Alexa starts the engine. "I see your point. Okay, you're in; we'll split the fee fifty-fifty. If I'm right, they're planning to explode the bombs at the mean high tide, to maximize the damage."

Linda's eyes dart back and forth. "That's... not until tomorrow, dawn."

"Oh? Hmmm... maybe my meddling has forced them to advance their timetable. Anyway, let's go!"

She revs the engine and races out of the harbor.

Meanwhile, in a stone cliff overlooking the harbor, Greg stands next to a jeep and looks toward the harbor with binoculars. A column of smoke rises from the warehouse. Next to him are three soldiers. He lowers the binoculars and looks at them.

"Get on the radio. Get boats and helicopters out here; we've got the rebel leader trapped."

At the same time, in Ocean Park on Eagle Island, An open expanse of grass dotted with a few trees, a small bandstand, a cement pond and a flowerbed, an art festival is in full swing. Makeshift walls have been strung all around, and works of art: watercolors, oils etc. hang on them. People mill about. Arthur, Silvana and Katrina stand near several oil paintings; all bear Silvana's signature.

"Good turnout, wouldn't you say?" Silvana says.

Arthur nods. "Splendid, best ever. Don't worry; I'm sure you'll still take the blue ribbon."

"Oh, that's not important."

Katrina frowns. "Just so long as you beat dumb Mrs. McCarthy! Every time she wins, I have to listen to Lisa gloat about it for the rest of the summer."

RING! All three reach for their cellphones. Arthur sees that it's his ringing and answers it. Silvana and Katrina put theirs away.

"Hello?"

Meanwhile, Alexa races along in her boat as Linda looks over several nautical charts.

"Pop, it's me. You in the lab? We need some help here."

"No, but I can get there lickety-split. Hold on! Got to go, ladies, sorry."

He takes off. Silvana rolls her eyes.

"Arthur, can't you ever-"

Kelly, flanked by three men dressed like Secret Service Agents, steps around the edge of a wall.

"Learn to relax?"

Silvana looks confused. "What? Oh, hello, don't believe I've had the pleasure. You a patron of the arts?"

"Yes, quite. Kelly Delaney, I met with your husband and daughter a few days ago."

"And you're still able to smile after that?" Katrina asks.

Silvana frowns. "Katrina!"

Kelly laughs. "Quite all right. I have a big sister too; so I know what kind of jerks they can be."

"Thank you for understanding, and excusing my daughter's ill manners!"

Katrina turns away and mimes gagging.

"Not at all. They spoke of your lovely island and its quaint customs, like the art festival. So, I thought I might come up and see it."

Katrina eyes the guards. "Ahhh... and what do they do, carry your luggage?"

"A woman in my position has to take precautions."

The guards move to take up strategic positions around the women.

At the same time, Arthur rushes into his lab, phone to his ear and starts to operate equipment. He looks at a viewscreen.

"Okay, I'm tracking you, kiddo. So, where do you need to get to?"

Alexa turns to Linda. "Linda, your call; where to?"

Linda slaps a chart down next to the steering wheel and points at a spot. "If I'm right, and I'm pretty sure I am, if we disable the bomb here, it'll turn that tsunami into a tiny wave."

Alexa punches some numbers into her equipment. "Okay, Pop, the location is coming through to you now. My navigational equipment is damaged, so I need you to guide us there."

Arthur looks at the screen. "You got it. Steer north northwest."

Meanwhile, back in Aqua Grande Harbor, Four military boats race out of the harbor. Above them four military helicopters follow; Greg in the lead one.

A short time later, in an open expanse of the ocean marked by a single buoy, Alexa's boat sits tied to the buoy. Linda comes up from down below, decked out in full scuba gear.

"You sure about this?" Alexa asks.

"Yes, if you're sure about everything you told me."

"I am."

"Then our only chance at disarming this thing, without tripping the alarm, is down there."

"Okay, just make it fast. I get the feeling we're going to have company, real soon!"

Linda gives her a thumb's up, sets her gear and moves to the side. SPLASH! Over she goes. Alexa switches on her communicator.

"Okay, Pop, we're on it. Everything there okay?"

"Well... we do have... company. Miss Delaney showed up at the art festival."

"Uh-oh! Let me guess, she's not alone."

"Why, that's right! How'd you know?"

"Lucky guess. Where is she now, and where are mom and Katrina?"

"At the festival; you know your mother."

"Yeah, unfortunately. Pop, get back there and get them away from her!"

"What? Alexa, you're being paranoid. She's not going to try anything there, not in front of all those people."

"I wouldn't be too..." Alexa looks off toward the horizon. The military boats and helicopters race along, searching. "Uh-oh. Pop, got to go, company's coming, and I got to put on my Sunday best! Listen, you've got to get mom and Katrina away from that woman. But, be subtle about it. You go charging in there, she's going to get suspicious. Got it?"

"Of course. When have I ever been heavy-handed about things?"

Alexa rolls her eyes. "You want that list alphabetically, or by degree of importance? Bye!" She ends transmission. She pops open a secret compartment and pulls out her Super eagle costume. "Time for action!"

In his lab, Arthur paces about, rubbing the back of his neck and runs his fingers through his hair. "Think-think-think. How can I-? Wait a minute."

He looks over and sees his cellphone. Snatching it up, he grabs his binoculars and heads for the window. He looks out at Ocean Park below, then puts the binoculars aside and starts to send a text message. When done, he puts the phone aside and looks out with the binoculars again.

Meanwhile, a military helicopter, high-powered aircraft, sleek and efficient, and loaded with weapons flies along. Greg sits next to the pilot and looks out over the ocean with binoculars. Slowly, he turns his head, scanning the area. He freezes and then points.

"There, about nine o'clock! I see his boat."

Greg sees Alexa's boat tied up to the buoy. A dark mass passes in front of him, momentarily obscuring his view. He lowers his binoculars.

"Huh, what was-?"

BAM! The helicopter shakes as it's hit by a small bomb.

"Monster!" cries the pilot.

He points out the window. Greg looks. Super Eagle whizzes by. The other helicopters maneuver to fire at her as she drops bombs on the boats below.

"What the-? Is this a joke? We got us some kind of crazy birdman here!"

Super Eagle zips about, trying to disable the boats and helicopters. They fire rockets and guns at him, but miss. Unfortunately, they sometimes hit each other! Three boats explode, bursting into flames. Three choppers go down, and some of their crews manage to bail out. Greg's chopper is damaged and is forced to land in the water. He climbs out and is picked up by the remaining boat. Super Eagle flies off, away from Alexa's boat and becomes a dot on the horizon. She then swoops low over the water and doubles back to her boat.

"Forget the flying freak! Come on, get to that boat," Greg says.

The boat races toward Alexa's boat. Greg pulls out his cellphone and dials, and then pulls his binoculars up to his eyes and looks toward Alexa's boat.

Back in Arthur's lab, he lowers his binoculars. "Come on, Silvana, read it!"

In Ocean Park, Silvana pulls out her phone and sees that she's got a text message. She puts it away.

"Anything wrong?" Kelly asks.

"Just a message. Probably Arthur telling me he won't be back for the judging. That man and his work!"

Kelly's cellphone rings, she answers it.

At the same time, Arthur kicks the cabinet in his lab. "Oh, that woman and her art!" He paces back and forth, stops and grabs his phone. "Ah, got it. No teenager can resist a text message!"

A moment later, Katrina's phone beeps. She pulls it out and sees that she's got a text message. She punches it up and reads it as Kelly talks in the background.

"I see. So, you feel action is needed?" Kelly asks.

Katrina's eyes get bigger and bigger. She looks at Silvana, happily chatting with one of the guards. She looks at Kelly, who stares at her like a bug under a microscope. She looks at the other guards, all moving closer. She swallows hard and starts to tug on a bit of her hair. Kelly gestures to the guards, and they move closer.

Meanwhile, back in the ocean, Linda surfaces, pulls off her fins and tosses them onboard. "Alexa, I did it!"

She swims to the ladder and starts to climb aboard. Alexa pops up, looking down at her with a big grin.

"Excellent! Glad to hear one of us had something to do. I've just been sitting here twiddling my thumbs."

She helps Linda get onboard.

"Well, I couldn't have done it without you! So, let's head for the next one. Even one of those things going off is too many; they'll devastate the ecosystem down there."

Alexa nods. "I agree. Let's-uh-oh. Honey, get out the good silverware, we got company!"

Linda turns. Standing not far away is the military boat, its guns trained on them. Greg stands up at the bow.

"Morning, Miss Mayhew, Miss Hart; fancy running into you two out here?"

Alexa smiles. "Just doing a bit of deep sea fishing."

"Any luck?"

"Nope, not the right kind of bait. If you want to catch a bottom-dweller, you need something they like. Care to volunteer?"

Greg laughs. "Ah, ever the funny girl. I take it Miss Hart is responsible for our little 'toy' going offline?"

"You know us women, not mechanically inclined at all. We'll get you something new when we get back to port. How about some handcuffs and a prison costume?"

"Sorry, the 'little woman' wouldn't approve. So, Miss Hart, if you'd be good enough to go down and fix it?"

Linda shakes her head. "I don't think so."

"Miss Mayhew, explain the real world to her; she has visions of dolphins and whales living in harmony with people in bubble cities."

Alexa smiles. "I know that one; 'Sealab 2020', right? I watched it as a kid."

Linda frowns. "Look, if you two could cut the bull for a minute; I know what you want, and it's not going to happen. What, you'll kill us if I don't? Then who'll fix your gadget? Besides, you're going to kill us anyway."

"My goodness, for a starry-eyed environmentalist, you are logical! However, I do have a trump card. Alexa, if you'll check your phone; you're about to get a call."

Alexa's phone beeps. She checks it, a photo is being sent to her. She punches it up and sees Katrina and Silvana standing between to guards. Katrina looks scared.

"Who are they? Oh, your family!" Linda asks.

"Yes."

Greg grins. "So, do we have a deal?"

"I won't ask, Linda. It's your choice," Alexa says softly.

"I'll do it," Linda says.

Back at Ocean Park, Silvana continues to happily chat with Kelly, totally oblivious to what's going on. The guards hem her and Katrina in.

Katrina looks around, desperation on her face. She looks down at her phone and smiles. She starts to surreptitiously send a text message. Nearby, three of her friends get text messages. They start to converge on Silvana and Katrina.

At the same time, Alexa sits, bound hand and foot, with her back to the water. Greg and a soldier stand before her, grinning.

Greg checks his watch. "So, just a few more minutes, and we can run along. I got to ask, why?"

Alexa paints an innocent look on her face. "Why what?"

Greg rolls his eyes. "Oh, please."

"Oh, all right, I'll stop playing hard to get. My parents raised me to be concerned for this tiny world of ours."

"Oh, a couple of Greenies, huh? Got your head in the clouds, girl. We can squeeze this world for every dime it's worth! Why throw that away?"

"Guess I'm just not that bright."

Greg and the soldier laugh.

"You got that right!"

By now, the four teens have moved in on all sides of Silvana, Katrina, Kelly and the guards. Two of the teens go around to the other side of the wall that they're all standing in front of. The two look through a crack in the wall. The other two teens nod. With a mighty heave, they push. The wall collapses, knocking two of the guards down. A third teen snatches a painting off another wall and whacks Kelly over the head with it. A guard grabs Silvana. Katrina pulls him off of her, and then they all take off.

"Katrina, what's going on?" Silvana asks.

"We'll explain later, Mom. Come on, we've got to get home!"

They race from the park. Kelly and the guards get to their feet and give chase. Katrina flips open her phone and dials.

"Pop, we're out of here, and we need help! Call the constable."

Now, Linda, is tied up, and sits next to Alexa. The soldier starts the engine of the military boat. Greg stands in front of Alexa and Linda.

"Thank you, Miss Hart, for your cooperation. As per our agreement, I'll call off Miss Delaney and her goons."

Greg dials on his cellphone, a smug smile on his face. Slowly, it changes to a frown.

Alexa grins. "'Can you hear me now? Can you hear me now?' Forgot to pay your bill?"

"A slight technical difficulty, nothing more."

Alexa laughs. "I'll bet. I know that 'technical difficulty', she's my sister!"

Greg hops in the other boat. "Doesn't matter. It just means you have to sit there and wonder if your family is safe. Enjoy the show!"

"So, you really are going to leave us here to die?" Linda asks.

Greg nods. "Those cables could hold an elephant. Besides, I'd like them to... relish their final remaining hour on this world."

The soldier starts the engine, he drives the boat away.

Linda looks out over the water. "Beautiful sea, isn't it? I suppose, if I have to die, I couldn't ask for a better place."

Alexa starts to wiggle and flex her muscles. "Don't give up just yet, Linda. I've still got a few tricks up my sleeve."

CHAPTER 5
A FIERY ENDING

SNAP! Alexa breaks free and stands up. She works to untie Linda.

"Wow, some trick there, 'Miss Houdini'. Got any more? Because they took all the tools and scuba gear. So, there's no way we're disabling this nuke."

Alexa moves to the bow and raises the anchor. "Yes, but they didn't smash the engine."

"Meaning we can leave. And then what?"

"You said this nuke was the key. We disarm or move it, and the tidal wave amounts to nothing."

"Move?" Linda asks, and then looks at the anchor. "But that would mean... Yes, let's do it."

Meanwhile, back in the Mayhew living room, Silvana, Katrina and the teens burst into the room through the front door. They slam and lock it behind them, and start to barricade the door with anything they can find.

Arthur dashes in from the other room and embraces Silvana. The teens take up positions around the door and watch out the windows.

"Would someone please explain what's going on here?" Silvana asks.

"One thing at a time, Mom. Pop, did you call the constable?"

Arthur nods. "Yeah, but he and his deputy are doing crowd control for the art festival. It's going to be a while before they can get here."

Katrina smiles. "Yeah, but Dippy Delaney doesn't know that! I bet she and her goon squad are already taking off."

"Good," Arthur says. "You all keep watch, I'm going to go call Alexa, see how things are on her end."

Out on the open expanse of the Pacific, military ships and helicopters smolder and burn, surrounded by floating debris. Alexa slowly maneuvers the boat in amongst the wreckage of the military boats and helicopters. Linda gathers what weapons she can find on the port side. The buoy, tied to the anchor line, bangs against the starboard side. BEEP-BEEP! The communicator beeps. Alexa switches it on.

"Hey, Pop, how's it going? Give me good news!"

Arthur stands at his equipment and looks at the view screen. Katrina stands off to the side.

"Yes, the news is very good; your mother and sister are fine. From what they've told me, Katrina was quite resourceful."

Alexa laughs. "Ah, I knew "Bratina" would live up to her name."

Katrina bolts to the screen. "I heard that!"

"Oh, boy. Pop, next time, warn me when she's around."

"Take it back, or I'm telling mom!"

"Pop, this is code red; I really need to talk to you!"

"Katrina, please, run along, I'll deal with your sister later."

"No-no-no! She apologizes, or else," Katrina whines.

Arthur pushes a series of buttons. "I guess we'll go with 'or else'."

Katrina shoots straight up and sticks to the ceiling.

"Heyyyyy!" she cries.

"Now, you just wait on the ceiling until we're done, okay?"

"The ceiling? Pop, what did you-?" Alexa asks.

"Just my new invention, a localized gravity inverter. It's not perfected, so you can't-"

Katrina gasps. "Not... perfected?"

"So, what do you need?" Arthur asks.

"These nukes, any idea of their range? How far would we have to move one in order to minimize its effect?"

Arthur scratches his head and paces a bit. "Hmmm... tough to say, all we have is the trigger to go by. Ideally, as far as possible. Realistically, at least twenty nautical miles. Why, what's going on there?"

Alexa and Linda look at each other. Alexa shakes his head.

"Just... improvising a solution, Pop. Don't worry about it. Do me a favor, tell Mom and... Katrina how much I love them."

"Ha, she said it!" Katrina says.

Arthur presses his lips together and opens his mouth, then closes it and turns away. He blinks away a tear, and turns back to the monitor.

"Sure, kiddo. I... good luck."

He switches off the monitor and slowly walks out.

"Ah, excuse me. Pop, I'm still up here. Help!"

Alexa steers the boat as it moves slowly along. Linda checks the weapons and tosses the broken ones on the deck. The buoy bangs into the side again and again as they go.

"You... sure you know what you're... doing?" Alexa asks.

Linda smiles. "Oh yeah. My dad's a former Green Beret who loves to hunt. I grew up on military bases, and I could hit a bull's eye by the time I was ten."

"Boy, I'm glad you're on my side!"

"Any chance of us going faster?"

Alexa shakes her head. "Nope. If I drive the engines any harder, they'll burn out. If we're lucky, we can just make it far enough, before they detonate this ugly sucker."

"Any chance of us getting... away?"

Alexa chews her lip. "Ah... maybe."

Linda looks off over the water. A few fluffy white clouds drift by and seagulls fly along. "At least... it's a beautiful day, and I'm out on the water. I couldn't ask for a better day to... be alive."

Meanwhile, the "Ocean's Quest" moves through the water. On the sleek, modern command center of the research vessel, Steve stands at the steering wheel. Greg is next to him, talking on the communicator. Kelly's face is on the viewscreen.

"Yes, we just left the island. That vile brat, Katrina, she somehow signaled her friends and... well, it doesn't matter; just so long as you're sure everything is on schedule."

Greg nods. "Absolutely! Steve and his boys repaired the other bomb, and I took care of the primary. We are at T-minus forty-two minutes, and counting."

"Excellent! Head to the safety point, then blow everything."

BEEP-BEEP! A tracking device next to Steve comes to life. He turns and looks at it.

"Ah... excuse me, folks, but we've got a problem. The primary is moving!"

Greg bolts over to the tracking device and studies the readings.

"B-but how?"

"Did you kill Alexa and Linda?" Kelly asks.

Well... not... exactly."

Steve frowns. "Not exactly killing someone is like not exactly brushing your teeth! You either do it, or you don't."

"Thank you, 'Mr. Science', I know that!" Greg snaps.

"Apparently, you don't!" Kelly growls.

Greg turns back to the communicator. "Miss Delaney, I left them tied up in cables that no one could possibly break, with knots even Alexander the Great couldn't unravel."

"Who?" Kelly asks.

Greg rolls his eyes. "You and your TV generation."

"Hey, check out the readings," Steve says. "They're moving all right, but real slow. We can catch them in no time. Give me... ten minutes, and we'll have them."

"Excellent!" Kelly says. "Find them, kill them, and get that bomb back where it belongs. You have less than forty minutes to do so."

The communicator clicks off, the screen going blank. Steve guns the engines. The "Ocean's Quest" races off, huge columns of water foaming up at its stern.

Meanwhile, a plush and expensive corporate helicopter flies away from Eagle Island. Kelly sits on a luxurious leather seat, flanked by two of her guards, while the third pilots the chopper. She lifts a briefcase onto her lap. She opens it. Inside is a computer control console and screen. The screen displays a series of flashing dots in the Pacific Ocean. All are blue, except one. She pushes a series of buttons, inserts a key in a slot and turns it. A red button lights up. She caresses it with her finger.

"Once they're all blue, we go boom. No witnesses, no proof. The 'Ocean's Quest' will be tragically lost at sea."

She smiles. The guards grin and slowly nod.

In the Mayhew living room, Arthur and Silvana watch as Kelly's helicopter flies off into the distance. The teens all smile.

"Looks like we're safe," Arthur says.

Silvana sighs. "Thank God. Hey, where's Katrina?"

Arthur rubs the back of his neck. "Katrina, Katrina... Hmmm, I just saw her hanging around somewhere. Now, where was that?"

Out on the open ocean, Alexa slows down and checks the starboard side of the boat.

"I'm going to have to slow down even more. The buoy is damaging the side too much. The bilge pump can't keep up."

"Great. One good-sized hole and down we go!"

Alexa looks off into the distance. She zooms in on the "Ocean's Quest" as it races toward them.

"You say you're a marksman with a gun?"

"No, I'm an expert with a rifle. Why?"

Alexa points off into the distance. "We just ran out of time."

Linda turns and looks where Alexa pointing. She squints, and then the "Ocean's Quest" starts to come into view. She grabs a rifle and kneels down at the stern.

"Time to kick ass, Alexa! You with me?"

"You got it!"

Linda looks at the buoy and the damage to the boat, then looks at Alexa.

"Punch it!"

Alexa revs the engine. "Hang on!"

She throws the boat into high speed and takes off. The buoy crashes again and again into the side, making the hole worse. The RPM gauge goes into the red. The "Ocean's Quest" closes in; Alexa swerves and turns, trying to not offer a sitting target. BANG! POW! Gunfire comes the "Ocean's Quest". Linda takes aim and fires back. Steve steers, racing the engines and closing in on Alexa's boat. Greg loads a rifle fitted with a sniper's scope. A thug races in and hides behind a console.

"What are you doing?" Steve asks.

"They're shooting back! You didn't say anything about them being armed. It's no fair them fighting back!"

Greg chambers a round. "Come on, you wimp, I'll finish this - now!"

The "Ocean's Quest" closes on Alexa's boat. Linda continues to fire at the thugs, they fire back. Alexa tries to get out of the way, but water is pouring in through the gaping hole in the hull. Smoke starts to billow out of the engine. Alexa beats on the control panel and turns to Linda.

"Honey, I think it's time for an oil change."

"You'll have to deal with it, 'dear', I'm having a little disagreement with the neighbors."

"I'll see what I can do."

Greg comes out on the deck of the "Ocean's Quest", kneels down and takes aim. He looks through the sniper scope and takes aim at Linda.

"Smile, sweetie, you're dead!"

Greg flips the safety off, and starts to squeeze the trigger. WHOOSH! A dark mass rushes by Greg. He flinches. BANG! He fires, and the bullet misses Linda, tearing a hunk out of the deck next to her. She looks up, sees Greg and fires at him. BAM! Greg's rifle is hit and damaged.

"Damn! What was that?"

A thug points up into the sky, his mouth hanging open. "Da-da..."

"What is your problem?"

Greg looks where he's pointing. Super Eagle flutters overhead and lands on the bow of the "Ocean's Quest".

Steve bolts out on deck. "Who-"

Greg stands. "The-"

The thus stands next to Greg. "Heck-"

"Is she?" Linda says.

Alexa hurls a handful or feather darts at the thugs nearest him. They stiffen, and then collapse to the deck.

"I am Super Eagle, Defender of Justice! Stop this, now."

Greg points at Alexa, then at Linda. "Kill her! And get her!"

Men charge Alexa, guns blazing. She explodes a smoke screen and takes off, zooming around behind them and knocks out several of them with his darts. Smoke engulfs Alexa's boat as the engine burns out and it slowly comes to a stop. Four thugs charge over the side of the "Ocean's Quest" and leap onto Alexa's boat. There are sounds of a struggle. The smoke clears, and the thugs are fighting each other, Linda is gone.

BANG! POW! Thugs, Steve and Greg fire at Alexa as she zooms about. She knocks out several more men, and then gets hit in the arm. She struggles to stay aloft. Linda pops up on the other side of the "Ocean's Quest" and climbs aboard. She slips onto the bridge. Steve stands at the railing and points at Alexa's boat.

"Never mind Linda Loser, untie the buoy and lash it to our side. We've got a schedule to keep!"

The four thugs untie the buoy and move it to the "Ocean's Quest" and lash it to the starboard side. BOOM! BAM! Alexa hurls small bombs at them in an effort to stop them. BANG! POP! More gunfire; Alexa is hit again, and she tumbles into the ocean and vanishes beneath the surface.

Greg raises a fist in triumph. "Yes, that is one dead duck!"

Linda, dripping wet, finishes sealing the doors of the bridge, and steps over to the throttle.

Steve looks out over the water as the thugs finish getting onboard.

"So, okay, let's get-"

VROOM! The ship takes off. Steve, Greg and the thugs are almost knocked off their feet.

"Who's driving this crazy boat?" Steve asks.

They turn and look through the windshield of the bridge. They see Linda, standing there, a smug smile on her face as she steers the ship away. Steve, Greg and the thugs start to pound on the door to the bridge.

"Some of you," Steve says. "Go around to the other side! Beat that door down, shoot the window out if you have to, but get in there."

Four of the men take off and move around to the door on the other side of the ship. Two thugs pick up rifles, load them and take aim at the windows of the bridge.

Meanwhile, Alexa's boat slowly settles in the water, sinking. Alexa hoists himself up onto the boat, blood on her costume. She looks around, and sees the "Ocean's Quest" racing away. She stands and pulls out a life raft. She pulls a cord and it inflates, and she pushes it off into the water. She spreads his wings, and takes off, flying after the ship.

"Not so fast, dudes, I bought a round-trip ticket for this cruise."

Linda spins the steering wheel from one side to the other in an effort to keep Steve, Greg and the thugs at bay. BANG! POW! SMASH! Two windows shatter. CRACK! The starboard door shudders and starts to give way. The wind howls in through the open windows, buffeting Linda. She clings to the wheel, trying to keep control.

"Give it up, sweetie; we're coming for you!" Steve says.

"You'll have to wait, dork-face, I just washed my hair and can't do a thing with it."

CRASH! The port door heaves inward, its upper hinge snapping off. Linda spins the wheel wildly, turns, and steps over to the Engineering Control Panel. She kicks at it, again and again. Two thugs leap through the smashed window and charge Linda. She turns and takes the first one down with a hard karate kick, then turns and kicks the panel again.

BZZZZZZ-BANG! The panel shorts out, and then explodes. The bridge is engulfed in smoke.

Alexa flies overhead. Steve and Greg bolt into the bridge, even as smoke billows out the broken windows. Alexa lands on the port side, near the stern. The thugs see her and charge her. They fight, and she knocks them out. She races toward the door to the bridge, even as Linda emerges from the smoke and runs smack into Alexa. They tumble to the deck.

"You, you're that Super Flier Girl!"

"Super Eagle, yes. Come on; let's get you out of here."

"What about Alexa?"

"She's in a life raft. I flew over her; she's fine. It's you I'm worried about now. So, hold on!"

BOOM! BAM! The stern heaves and cracks, flames shooting up from below the deck. Linda holds onto Alexa. She runs, jumps, and flies off. Greg emerges from the bridge, draws his pistol and takes aim at them.

"How many times do I have to kill her before she stays dead?

BANG! He fires, hitting Alexa in the back. BOOOMMM! The engines of the ship explode, the "Ocean's Quest" erupts into a massive fireball. The shockwave races out in all directions. Alexa struggles to stay aloft. The shockwave hits her and Linda. They go down. SPLASH! And vanish beneath the waves. Debris rains down all over the area. The ship breaks up, burns and slowly settles into the sea.

Bubbles rise to the surface. Linda bobs to the surface. She swims around, searching.

"Eagle Girl, where are you? Hello! Are you there? Is anyone there?"

Linda treads water and looks around. Behind her, Alexa paddles toward her in the lift raft.

"I'm here, Linda."

Linda spins around. "Alexa! You're... okay? No, you're hurt!"

Alexa winces in pain as she paddles. "It's... not bad, just flesh wounds."

Did you see that Eagle Girl?"

"Yes, she flew off toward the shore. She said she'd send help. But, it's okay; I got a GPS distress signal going. We've got a good chance of making it.

She reaches Linda, and helps her get into the raft.

Some days later, in a simple hospital room, Linda lies in bed, bandaged up and asleep. Alexa appears at the door, in a wheelchair, Arthur behind her.

"How's she doing?" Alexa asks.

"Surprisingly well. Considering her wounds, exposure, and the less than stellar state of medicine in this country! She should be fine."

"How much longer do I have to wear this stupid bandage and use this mini-race cart?"

"Just until we get to the airport and head home. The doctors saw your wounds, Alexa. You go walking around now and they'll get suspicious."

"Okay. All the other bombs taken care of?"

"Yeah, I did it under the cover of following up on Linda's research."

Alexa smiles. "So, we won. But, I got to wonder, what's Globe-Corp up to? What's next on their agenda?"

"Well, we'll have to keep an eye on them from now on."

Alexa reaches into her pocket and pulls out a huge bar of chocolate. "Two eyes. Hey, on the flight back, can we divert to Punta Gorda? I got a little present for an old friend."

Arthur laughs. "Sure. Now, come on, let's get you back to your room so you can 'rest' until we're ready to go."

"Okay. See you, Linda."

Alexa backs up. Arthur pushes her chair down the hall. Linda opens her eyes and sits up. She looks toward the door, a questioning look on her face.

THE END

TO THE READER

Too many superheroes these days are men. Here is an action hero who is a young woman, and she's dedicated to not only helping people, but protecting the environment. These days, issues like Global Warming are at the forefront of the news, and it's important that we pay attention to the potential dangers facing the future. Super Eagle does that, and yet is entertaining, funny, and exciting.

Printed in the United States
by Baker & Taylor Publisher Services